MITKO

GARTH GREENWELL

For Caroline —
who read this book with
immense openness, generosity,
+ care —

thank you for sharing
your very beautiful reading
with me —

With immense
gratitude —

Miami University Press
Oxford, Ohio

io April 2012

Susanee

Edited by David Schloss
Cover design by Madge Duffey
Book design by Dana Leonard

Library of Congress Cataloging-in-Publication Data

Greenwell, Garth.
 Mitko / by Garth Greenwell.
    p. cm.
  ISBN 978-1-4507-6214-4
1. Gay men--Fiction. 2. Americans--Bulgaria--Fiction.
3. Psychological fiction. I. Title.
 PS3607.R4686M57 2011
 813'.6--dc22
                      2011006163

Printed on acid-free paper in the United States of
America

FOR RICARDO MOUTINHO FERREIRA

THAT MY FIRST ENCOUNTER WITH MITKO B. involved a betrayal, even a minor one, should have given me greater warning at the time, which should in turn have made my desire for him less, if not eradicated it completely. But warning, in places like the bathrooms at the National Palace of Culture, where we met, is like some element coterminous with the air, ubiquitous and inescapable, so that it becomes a part of those who inhabit it, and thus part and parcel of the desire that draws us there. Even as I descended the stairs I heard his voice, which like the rest of him was too large for those subterranean rooms, spilling out of them as if to climb back into the afternoon, the bright afternoon that, though it was October already, had nothing autumnal about it, so that the grapes that hung ripe from vines throughout the city burst warm still in one's mouth. I was taken aback to hear them, two men talking unfurtively in a place where, by unstated code, voices seldom rose above a whisper.

The voices—only one of them, I realized now, fully raised, the other a low murmur—were clearly in the second of the bathroom's three chambers, where they might have been two men washing their hands had the sound of water accompanied them, and they were stationary, they didn't approach me as I turned down the short corridor toward the wc. Whatever their business, they were stationed there, which really left only one explanation, the bathrooms at NDK (as the Palace is called) having a single purpose only, any other use of them accidental; and yet this explanation seemed contradicted by the demeanor of the man who claimed my attention as I turned into the room, which was cordial and brash and entirely public in that place of intense and shared privacies.

He was tall, thin but broad shouldered, with the close-cropped military cut of hair so popular among young men here, young men who affect a hyper-masculine style and about whom there hangs an aura of criminality. I hardly noticed the man he was with, who was shorter, deferential, with bleached blond hair and a denim jacket from the pockets of which he never removed his hands. It was the larger man who turned toward me with an interest apparently friendly, free of either predation or fear, and without any of the veils we affect in seduction, even seductions as certain and brief as those transacted in these little rooms. I found myself smiling in response, and he greeted me with an elaborate rush of words, at which, as I grasped briefly in mine the large hand he held out to me, I could only shake my head bemusedly, offering as broken apology and defense the few phrases I had practiced to numbness. His smile widened when he realized that I was a foreigner, revealing a chipped front tooth, the jagged seam of which (I would learn) he worried obsessively with his index finger in moments of abstraction. Even at our present, unintimate distance, the smell of alcohol emanating not so much from his breath as from his clothes, his hair, the hand I shook, the very exhalations of his pores, was overwhelming and explained (as I thought) his strange freedom in that place that, for all its license, was bound by such inhibition; it explained, too, the peculiarly innocent quality of his gaze, which was intent now but unthreatening. He spoke again, cocking his head a little, and in a weird pidgin of Bulgarian, English, and German, we managed to establish that I was American, that I had been in his city for a few weeks, that I was a teacher at the American College, that I would be in the country for two years at least, that my name was more or less unpronounceable in his language.

Throughout this conversation, which was halting and punctuated by pauses and awkward gestures and trilingual stumbling, there was no acknowledgment of the strange location of our encounter or of the uses to which it was almost exclusively put, so that I felt, speaking to him, an anxiety made up of equal parts desire and unease at the mystery of his presence and purpose. There was a fourth man there, stationed in the farthest stall, which he entered and exited several times, looking at us intently but never approaching or speaking a word. Finally, after a pause in which we seemed to have reached the end of our ingenuity and after this fourth man had entered his stall again, closing the door behind him, Mitko (as I knew him now) pointed towards him and gave me a look of great significance, saying in Bulgarian "he wants" and then making a lewd gesture the meaning of which was clear. Both he and his companion, whom he referred to as *brat mi* and who hadn't spoken since I arrived, laughed at this, looking at me as if to include me in the joke, though, as of course they must have known, I was as much an object of their ridicule as that man with whom I would never exchange a word. Such was my eagerness to associate with them, to be one of their party, that as if by reflex I smiled and wagged my head from side to side in the gesture that signifies here both agreement or affirmation and a certain wonder at the vagaries of the world. But this betrayal didn't bring me closer to them or make me one of their party; instead, as I saw in the quick glance they exchanged, it increased the distance between us, and I suspected they even felt something like contempt for me now, though perhaps this was merely my own contempt, self-inspired. Trying to regain my footing, and after having taken a moment to arrange the necessary syllables in my head (which seldom, despite these efforts, emerge as they should, even now when

I'm told that I speak *hubavo* and *pravilno*, when I see surprise at my proficiency in a language that hardly anyone bothers to learn who hasn't learned it already), I asked him what he was doing there, in that chill room with its impression of damp. It was still just early fall, almost summer still, the plaza above us was full of light and people, some of them, riding skateboards or in-line skates or elaborately tricked-out bicycles, the same age as these men.

Mitko looked at his friend, whom he referred to as his brother although they were not brothers, and after they shared another meaningful glance the friend moved toward the outer door and Mitko drew his wallet out of his back pocket, opened it, and took out a small square packet of glossy paper, a page torn from a magazine folded over many times. He unfolded this page carefully, his hands shaking just slightly, balancing it so that whatever loose material was enclosed would not suddenly be lost to the dampness and filth on which we stood. I anticipated, of course, what he would reveal, and my only surprise was at the poverty of his supply, a mere crumble of leaves. Ten leva, he said, and then added (as if having scented a likelier desire) that he and his friend and I, the three of us, might smoke it together. He didn't seem overly disappointed when I refused this offer, he didn't, as I had feared, simply go elsewhere with his friend, seeking out a more promising market than this bathroom where the traffic was unusually light, perhaps because of the beautiful afternoon; he only folded his page carefully around its cargo again and replaced it in his pocket. His friend didn't rejoin us, but stayed at the entrance, not so much guarding it anymore as allowing us a certain privacy. I can't remember now how our conversation shifted finally to sex; certainly I wasn't the one who shifted it, even though sex was my purpose in making the short but inconvenient journey from Mladost, my outlying region, to the center, even though sex was the only reason anyone (except by accident) descended the long stairs to these rooms so much like a bunker or a cave. It had become more and more difficult over the course of our conversation, which involved so much silence and which couldn't have lasted more than five minutes, or ten, to imagine the desire I increasingly felt for this large and extremely drunk man having any prospect of satisfaction. As we spoke (though we spoke little), he had seemed in some mysterious way to withdraw from me; the longer we avoided any erotic proposal the more finally he seemed unattainable, not so much because of his beauty, although I found him beautiful, as for some still more forbidding quality, a kind of bodily sureness and ease bespeaking freedom from doubts and self-gnawings, from any squeamishness about existence. He had about him a sense simply of accepting his right to a measure of the world's beneficence, even as so evidently it was withheld him. It wasn't I, then, who shifted the conversation, but somehow, by some gesture perhaps, he led me to realize that if I wasn't interested in his drugs there might be something else on offer. There was nothing in his manner of seduction; what he offered was a transaction, though neither did any of his friendliness melt away when reflexively and without a moment's consideration I said no to him, at the same moment feeling sure I would regret my initial response. It was the answer I had always given to such proposals (which inevitably one receives in the places I frequent), not out of moral conviction but out of pride, a pride I already felt weakening as suddenly I realized (though the process was gradual) I had been shifted by the passage of time from one category of erotic object to another.

Even as I said the word, then, I felt myself refusing that initial refusal, and so, since he did finally turn to leave with his friend, shrugging a little at my response, I found myself calling *chakai chakai chakai*, wait wait wait, repeating the word quickly and in the precise inflection I had heard an old woman use at an intersection one afternoon when a stray dog made as if to wander into traffic. Mitko turned back at once, as docile as if our transaction had already been made; perhaps in his mind it was already a sure thing, as it was in mine, though I pretended (more for my own sake than for his) to suffer still some hesitation. As if to assert some dominance over the overwhelming desire I felt for him, I even affected a certain skepticism about the goods on offer, skepticism that I didn't really feel and of which even the facade melted away when he stepped into a stall and unbuttoned the fly of his jeans and I realized I would pay whatever price he quoted. I made as if to claim those goods immediately, having always been a terrible negotiator or haggler, my desire immediately legible, but Mitko held me off, not (at first) as I expected, to demand his payment in advance, but instead to return to the outer room and its line of porcelain sinks, all of them cracked and stained, where he insisted on cleaning himself before we proceeded. Then, with a bodily candor I ascribed to drunkenness but would come to recognize as an inalienable trait, he pulled the long tube of his cock free from his jeans and leaned over the bowl of the sink to wash it, skinning it back and wincing at the contact with water that only comes out cold. It was some time before he was satisfied, the first sign of a fastidiousness that would never cease to surprise me, given his poverty and the general squalor in which it forced him to live.

It wasn't until he returned that I finally asked his price for the act I wanted, which was ten leva until I unfolded my wallet and found only twenty leva notes, one of which he eagerly claimed. Really what did it matter, the sums were almost equally meaningless to me, especially when laid against the object with which we agreed for a moment to pretend they were commensurate, or not precisely with the object itself but with a certain time during which I would be allowed its use, by which I mean its enjoyment. I would have paid twice as much, and twice as much again, which is not to suggest that I had unlimited or even particularly ample resources but that in my own estimation this body, the enjoyment of which I was contracting to rent, seemed almost infinitely dear. It was astonishing to think that any number of these soiled bills, one of which I now passed to him, might make that body available to me, that after the simplest of exchanges I might simply reach out for it and find it wondrously in my grasp. I placed my hands under the tight shirt he wore, and he gestured me back so that he could remove it, undoing each of its buttons and then hanging it carefully on the hook of the stall door behind him. He was thinner than I expected, less defined, and the hair that covered his torso had been shaved to bare stubble, so that for the first time I realized how young he was (I would learn he was twenty-three) as he stood boyish and exposed before me, motioning me now forward again with the exaggerated courtesy some drunk men assume and that can precede, the thought even in my excitement was never far, equally exaggerated outbursts of rage. No such outburst marred my first meeting with Mitko, who surprised me then by leaning towards me and laying his mouth on mine, kissing me generously, unrestrainedly, and though I hadn't done anything to initiate or invite such contact it was welcome and I sucked eagerly on his tongue, which was antiseptic with alcohol. There was something dramatic in this passionate embrace, his pretending to be overcome with desire and my pretending to believe it, but ~~it wasn't~~ so

different from more typical encounters, where
our responses are never in any simple way our
own, where they are always balanced against the
responses, perceived or projected, of our partner,
and also against our own fears and enthusiasms,
our claims and generosities, our failures of nerve, so
that sincerity, authenticity, flees ever more swiftly
away from us, like a shadow that we ourselves cast
out. Always we desire too much or not enough,
and compensate accordingly.

The theatricality of Mitko's embrace signified,
if anything, probably just how little he desired our
encounter, and really I think that he was intoxicated
past the point of conceiving desire, though he could
still speak and walk; I would be amazed, later, to
see how much he could consume and still, at least
in these basic ways, be said to function. My own
embraces, as I say, were equally theatrical, though
it wasn't my desire but my credulity that was
counterfeit; indeed, in his presence now, pressed to
him, that desire was heightened when I caught for
the first time, beneath the more powerful and nearly
overwhelming smell of alcohol, his own scent,
which would become the greatest source of the
pleasure I took from him and which I would seek
out (at his neck and crotch, beneath his arms) on
each of our encounters, a kind of animal response
granting me finally (what I have always sought
in desire) a release from myself. Throughout the
entirety of our first, abbreviated encounter I sucked
thirstily at this scent, as if taking some necessary

nourishment at an inadequate source. It was this pleasure, found in the most primitive response, that saved me from remorse or recrimination just a few moments later, long before by any estimate he might have discharged that obligation incurred when he took a soiled twenty leva note from me, before the contracted time, which was never exact, was up, and before I had had my fill of that fruit it amazed me to find I could reach out and claim without any resistance for myself, he made a strange loud sound and tensed himself, placing both of his palms flat against the sides of the stall. It was a poor performance of an orgasm, if that's what it was, not least because for the few minutes I had worked him he had shown no response at all, alcohol (as I imagined) having carried him beyond all reach of desire. Nonetheless, and despite my protests, he withdrew from me, and with the same courtesy motioned me back as he put on again the shirt he had hung so carefully behind him. I watched him helplessly, still kneeling, as he called out to his friend, whom he called again *brat mi* and who called back to him from the outer chamber. Perhaps he saw that I was angry, as (though only for a moment) I was, and wanted to remind me that he wasn't alone. Straightening his clothes, running his hands down his torso to settle them correctly upon his frame, he smiled at me (entirely without guile, as though perhaps he did feel that he had discharged his obligation), unlatched the door and pulled it shut again behind him. Still kneeling there, still tasting the metallic trace of the sinkwater from his skin, I found my anger already easing as I realized that in fact my pleasure was not abridged by his absence, that it was not even lessened. Instead, as the intensity of present experience dimmed and became, already processed by memory, approachable, even malleable, I found my pleasure actually heightened, so that what was surely a betrayal (we had our contract, no less binding for having never been signed, never set in words at all) became a refinement of our encounter, allowing him to become more vividly present to me even as I was left alone on my stained knees, and allowing me, with all the freedom of fantasy, to make of him what I would.

I sought out Mitko repeatedly over the next weeks, feeling an almost unbearable excitement as I approached NDK and, if I found him absent, suffering a sense of disappointment bordering almost on despondency. It was after our third or fourth encounter that I decided finally to invite him to my apartment. I wanted to have him, as it were, to myself, free of the audience we so frequently had at NDK, where men would hover outside the stall door or press their faces to its walls, trying to participate by means of stray sounds in whatever activities they were excluded from, as I also had done on finding myself among the unchosen. Increasingly I desired a greater privacy with Mitko, a greater intimacy and the luxury of time. But I was uneasy, too, and recognized the foolishness of inviting this stranger into my home, a stranger, moreover, steeped in a criminality that was part of his appeal. I remembered the warning of a man who had invited me, after a brief encounter, to take a coffee with him in the

Reinaldo
Arenas

large café in the main building of the Palace. These
boys, he said to me, you can't trust them, they
will find out about you, they will tell your work,
your friends, they will rob you—and indeed I had
been robbed, once successfully and once I caught a
man's hand as he withdrew it from my pocket, after
which he stared wild-eyed at me, the poor boy, and
fled. The rest of this man's warning fell on deaf
ears, as there's so little that would be destroyed by
such revelations—no one would feel betrayed, no
architecture of a life would be marred by the telling
of secrets that I air here anyway, where anyone can
find them if they have a mind to; I've never been
good at concealing anything, the whole bent of my
nature is toward confession. But the warning came
back to me nonetheless when Mitko and I finally,
on our third or fourth meeting (all more satisfying
than the first), exchanged phone numbers and set
up a date for the following evening. We had already
had sex; it was afterwards, sitting on a bench in
the sunlight, which was still warm though it was
November now and the season had turned, the
grapes had shriveled on their vines, that I decided
to return to the bathrooms below and to offer him
my proposal. He agreed eagerly enough, and it was
when he gave me his number, which I entered into
the electronic device I carried for such purposes,
pulling it out of my pocket for the first time in
his presence, that his eyes lit up with an acquisitive
gleam and I remembered, as Mitko held the little
device and scrolled through its various features and

screens, the warning I had received.

But this unease wasn't enough to set me off my purpose, and the next afternoon after classes I hurried downtown. We met again at NDK, where I found him in a huddle with three or four other men at the wall furthest from the entrance, all of whom straightened to attention and scattered when I appeared, though I didn't approach them and stood awkward at the threshold. Mitko, who had his back to me, turned immediately and smiled, offering me his hand and at the same time directing me out of the little room and away from his friends (if they were his friends), leading us both toward the upper air. As we walked up the long staircase, away from those rooms that had always seemed to me inadequate for him, his frame and voice and apparent eagerness for friendship all hemmed in by the damp tile of the walls, I felt, along with the excitement I had anticipated, an utterly unexpected happiness. He smelled of alcohol, if not of the same saturation as during our first meeting, and as we were walking through the park at NDK he showed me the knuckles of his right hand, which were skinned and raw, the wounds still fresh. He said that he had gotten into a fight with another hustler down below, though the reasons for it remained unclear to me. I took his hand in mine for a moment, looking at these little wounds that made him at once fierce and damaged, inviting care, and I imagined how I would salve them, rubbing them with ointment and then pressing them to my lips.

Nothing in our encounters gave me warrant for such tenderness, nothing except my own imaginings and the sweetness Mitko occasionally showed, always unexpectedly and always thrillingly, juxtaposed as it was against the brutality that was never far from him and that he revealed again now, reenacting his fight with quick jabs in the air. We walked quickly down Vasil Levski Boulevard, his long legs devouring the pavement so that I had to struggle to keep up with him, and Mitko talked the whole way, only bits of his narration available to me. For the first time I asked him where he lived and he answered *s priyateli*, with friends, a term that he used often and that I was never sure how to interpret, since in addition to its usual meanings Mitko used this word to refer to his clients. It became clear to me slowly, as I struggled to understand this stream of talk (frequently punctuated with *razbirash li?*, do you understand?), that Mitko shuttled between places, sometimes sleeping with these friends, sometimes (or so it seemed) walking the streets until morning. He had recourse, in inclement weather, to a little garret room to which a friend had given him the key, where there was a bed but no heat or running water.

It was clear that talking of these things made Mitko uneasy, and he changed the subject by saying that, though I had found him at NDK, where he had spent much of the day, he had nevertheless been saving himself for our encounter. He looked at me sidelong as he said this (*razbirash li?*) and I felt myself flush with pleasure and excitement. Mitko seemed eager, too, he seemed full of an energy that propelled him forward, and as we walked down Vasil Levski toward Graf Ignatief, crossing innumerable little streets and alleyways, more than once I had to grab his arm and, saying to him again *chakai chakai chakai*, pull him back from oncoming traffic. If he was indifferent to the dangers of the road, however, he was preternaturally attuned to the signs of material privilege. Repeatedly he paused to admire a passing jacket or pair of shoes, and as we turned finally onto Graf Ignatief he stopped for long moments at each of the many electronics stores, cell phone kiosks, and pawn shops, evaluating the products laid out in their displays. I was taken aback by how much he knew about these little trinkets, his monologues punctuated by English words for the various devices' specs, pixels and memory cards and battery life, information he must have gleaned from the advertisements and brochures he picked up everywhere they were offered. I found myself growing increasingly uncomfortable, both impatient to get home and uneasy at what seemed (more and more aggressively) like hints, especially as Mitko told me that his current phone, a model he clearly hoped to upgrade, was a gift from one of his friends. This word, *podaruk*, gift, would repeat again and again in Mitko's conversation that evening, applied at some point, it seemed, to nearly everything he owned. It's difficult for me to remember now precisely why these comments were so distressing to me. Perhaps I felt dismay at any reminder of the material basis of our friendship, which was so easy for me otherwise to forget, imagining that we seemed innocuous as any two men headed somewhere, friends or colleagues or even lovers; I wanted to pretend that nothing in our bearing toward each other revealed either his financial motivations or my risible desires. And perhaps I felt, even then, that these mercantile desires on Mitko's part were as bottomless as my own longings, that certainly I couldn't satisfy them, though I might be tempted to try.

We were walking down Graf Ignatief now, and as we approached the little river (really little more than a drainage ditch) that circles central Sofia, Mitko thrust his bag out for me to take and told me to wait for a moment, stepping off the sidewalk toward the sparse vegetation at the river's bank. I walked on a few steps, turning then to look back at him, whom I could just barely make out (it was dark now, the autumn night had fallen as we walked) standing at the bank to relieve himself into the water. He seemed entirely unconcerned by the passers-by, the heavy traffic on one of Sofia's busiest streets; he was blithely unselfconscious, and catching me watching him, he stuck his tongue out and wagged his cock in his hand, sending his piss in high arcs over the water, where it glimmered for a moment in the light of oncoming cars. It was a gesture so innocent, so full of childlike irreverence, that I found myself smiling stupidly back at him, filled with a sense of goodwill that buoyed me toward the metro station and our short commute. There is a single metro line in Sofia (though more are planned and great gouges have been opened throughout the city), and during peak hours, as I suppose is the case in any sizable city, it seems as though the entire population is shuttling underground, alternately swallowed and belched forth through the closing doors. There were no seats on the Mladost train, and Mitko and I found ourselves shuffled away from each other, standing finally a good ways apart in the press of bodies. Mitko studied the little maps above each set of doors, watching the stations light up as we passed them, but every now and then he glanced at me, as if to make sure I was still there or (more likely) that my attention was still fixed on him, and his look now wasn't innocent, anything but; it was a look that singled me out, a look full of promise, and under its heat I felt myself gripped yet again by both pleasure and embarrassment, and by an excitement so terrible I had to look quickly away.

When we emerged at the subway's last stop, Mladost 1, spilling with the other passengers onto Alexander Malinov Boulevard, I was surprised to see that Mitko knew the area well. Once he had oriented himself, he pointed toward one of the *blokove*, the dire Soviet apartment complexes that line both sides of the boulevard, and said that it was the home of one of his *priyateli*, a man with whom he had spent a good deal of time. As was always the case during our time together, I was frustrated by the fragments that were all I could glean from his stories, both because of my poor Bulgarian and because he kept speaking in a kind of code, so that I seldom understood precisely the nature of the relationships he was describing or why they ended as they did. Never before had I met anyone who combined such transparency (or the semblance of transparency) with such mystery, so that he seemed at once vulnerable, over-exposed, and unrelievedly hidden behind impervious defenses. We fell strangely silent as we walked toward my building, both of us perhaps thinking of what awaited us there. On my street, the relative prosperity of which marked it off from its neighbors, Mitko turned into a little shop for alcohol and cigarettes, a place I stopped at frequently and where I was known by the three people who shared responsibility for tending it. Mitko walked in before me, immediately placing both of his hands palm down on the glass counter, making the shopkeeper wince, and then leaned over to peer at the more expensive bottles where they were displayed on the back wall. He examined several of these, asking the man repeatedly and to his increasing exasperation to pass them over the counter so he could read their labels. In my pre-coital generosity I didn't balk at the exorbitant result of these deliberations, or at the cheap orange soda he chose to accompany it. Satisfied with these purchases, he carried them the three flights to my apartment, a two-bedroom affair provided by

my school, a fact I tried to communicate to him
when it became clear he thought I owned it. I don't
have that kind of money, I told him, relieved to
establish the modest reality of my means, a reality
he greeted with skepticism, even disbelief. But
you're American, he said, opening the door to
the little balcony that all apartments here have,
all Americans have money. I protested, telling
him I was a schoolteacher, that I made hardly any
money at all; but of course it made sense he would
think this, having seen my laptop computer, my
cellular phone, my iPod, emblems of comfort if
not particularly of wealth in America that here are
objects of some luxury. He stood on the balcony
a bit, holding his large tumbler of gin and orange
soda, and looked out over the little street where I
live, which seems never to have been given a name.
This is a curious feature of my quarter, these streets
without names, so different from the memorializing
impulse evident everywhere in the center, where
the nation's whole history, its victories and griefs,
the many indignities and small prides of a small
country, are played out in the names of its avenues
and squares. In Mladost, it's the *blokove*, the huge
towers, that anchor one in space, each with its
own number individually marked on city maps.
As he looked out on this street, nameless like its
neighbors, I asked Mitko what it was he did for
a living, by which I meant what it was he had
done, before he turned for whatever reason to his
priyateli. He was smoking a cigarette, that was why

he was on the balcony, though as the night wore on this consideration would lapse and the next morning I would wipe from the floor small piles of gray ash. He conveyed to me (largely in gesture) that he worked in construction, mimicking with his wounded hands the motions of his trade, going so far even as to walk a few steps as he would on a high beam, balancing against the wind. It took me a moment to realize that these movements, which were strangely familiar to me, were the same as those with which my father, in my childhood, often made us laugh as he recounted the single summer he spent working construction in Chicago, fresh from his farm in Kentucky, earning his tuition for law school and thus, among other things, purchasing my life.

It was then that Mitko told me he was from Varna, a beautiful port city on the Black Sea Coast and one of the centers of the astonishing economic boom Bulgaria briefly enjoyed, a boom that, here as in so much of the rest of the world, collapsed suddenly and seemingly without warning, someone having noticed finally the imaginary nature of its fuel. There were good years, Mitko said, he made good money, and with a strange urgency (it was here that the cigarette came inside) he dragged me from the balcony toward the table where I had stationed my computer. Opening it up, unfolding the little screen from the body, he made a sound of dismay at the state in which it was kept, the screen mottled with dust; *mrusen*, he said, dirty, with the same tone of voice he would use in response to the requests I would make of him later, requests expressive of those parts or portions of myself I air least frequently and with most shame, a tone of voice mocking and disapproving but also indulgent, spotting a fault it was in his power either to exploit or to repair. It was the latter he set about now, opening two cupboards and then a third before I understood what he was seeking and fetched the bottled cleaner from beneath the sink. He set his drink (the large glass almost empty) on the table beside him and dragged the computer into his lap, almost cradling it, and with a dampened tissue he began cleaning the screen, not in a desultory hurried way, as I might when finally I bothered, but taking his time, working at the stubborn corners, aiming for an immaculacy I would never think of needing. He then turned to the keyboard, almost as dirty as the screen; then he closed the machine and with his fifth or sixth tissue wiped down the aluminum case. *Sega*, he said with satisfaction, Now, and set the machine back on its perch, having done me a service in no way covered by our tacit contract. He reopened the computer then and navigated to a popular Bulgarian website, a kind of adult social networking site that I knew was a primary means of contact between gay men here. He had a profile there, and it was this he wanted to show me, or rather the pictures there, which he enlarged until they filled the screen. This was two years ago, he said as I looked at the young man in the image, who stood on Vitosha Boulevard with a bag from one of the posh stores there, his face full to the camera and smiling broadly at whoever held it, showing his unbroken teeth. It was difficult to recognize the man in the image as the man beside me; not only was the tooth unbroken, but also his head was unshaved, his hair brown and prosperous, conventionally cut. There was nothing rough or threatening about him at all; he looked like a nice kid, a kid I might have taught at the expensive school where I work. It was difficult to listen to him as he continued speaking, as I found myself strangely unnerved, unable to reconcile the change so short a time had wrought. It was hardly possible they could be the same, this prosperous teenager and the man beside me; and since I couldn't reason how a single life might accommodate them both I found myself wondering which life was real, which face (I looked repeatedly from one to the other) was the true face, and how it had been lost or gained.

Mitko, however, wasn't interested in the face of the young man in the picture, but rather in his dress. Look, he said, rattling off the names on the labels of what seemed to me fairly nondescript items of clothing: jeans, a jacket, a pull-down shirt; also a belt; also a pair of sunglasses. He even remembered the shoes he was wearing that day, though they weren't visible on the screen; perhaps they were special shoes, or perhaps it was a special day. *Hubavi*, he said, a word that means lovely or nice, and then, fingering the collar of his shirt, *mrusen*, so that I felt again a great up-welling of sympathy for him, and also of something else, since he pulled the offensive shirt off and turned back bare-chested to the screen. I leaned forward then (I had seated myself next to him) and kissed his shoulder, a chaste kiss, an expression of my sorrow for him, perhaps, though it wasn't exactly sorrow that I felt. Regardless, he looked at me, smiling broadly, the same smile as in the photograph or almost the same, though they looked nothing alike, one transformed—it's astonishing how thoroughly—by the broken tooth, its evidence of something undergone. He smiled and bent his head towards mine, but not to engage in the kiss I expected; instead, in a quick surprise, playfully and without any hint of seduction he licked the tip of my nose, turning then immediately back to his task. There were more photographs, several more, the young man featured in shifting scenes: here at the seaside, here in the mountains, always in the same casually prosperous dress of which he was so proud, the generic uniform of affluent young Americans, the stuff of endless racks in endless suburban malls. Then there were photographs in which he wore nothing at all, angling himself in postures of erotic display difficult to reconcile with the sweetly innocent gesture he had just made, so that still I felt myself baffled by contradictions I was unable to resolve, contradictions that, as they alternate and repeat and thus form patterns and reliances, as much as anything else make up the self. And yet even as we recognize and treasure this in ourselves, our evasions of easy accountings, this incoherence in others unnerves or offends us, forcing us to wonder which of the faces turned to us is the real face and which the subterfuge, which the essential and which the accident. In one of these photos which Mitko displayed he was lying on a bed, angled on one side so that he faced the camera, fully extending the length of his long body, or so it seemed, the image cut off just above his knees. He was hard, and one of his hands angled this, too, toward the lens, the focus and centerpiece of his advertisement. He wasn't smiling now, but instead bore a face locked in the seriousness demanded by such sites, these markets purveyed with such urgency or despair, their very richness creating dearth, so that one scrolls through image after image until one's eyes ache with fatigue and one's being with unsatisfied want. Still, even without that smile there was an intensity to his gaze that convinced me this camera, too, was held by someone significant, someone who elicited his look; and the effectiveness of the advertisement (were I scrolling through images I would have paused, I would have wondered about this man and thus begun my fantasy) was precisely this gaze, which, though it was not meant for any of the men who might be scrolling through these pages, still we could claim for ourselves. And indeed there was someone behind the camera, the next frame showed him, a young man of Mitko's height and build, with the same style of hair and the same dress. They were fully clothed, which made somehow only more erotic the embrace caught in the image, their attention focused wholly on each other, or so it seemed; there was no one behind the camera now; it was held by Mitko, one of whose arms extended weirdly toward us, toward me and that other Mitko as we together gazed at him. His other arm was wrapped around his partner, both of whose arms in turn gripped him, so that they seemed balanced in desire, in their urgency and their hunger for each other. It was tempting to think there was nothing theatrical about this kiss, that the evaluating, doubting, haggling self had dissolved at that point where their mouths opened to each other, releasing them from that tormenting consciousness that never lets us alone; and yet it wasn't free of theater, and the very lens that allowed me access to it, in fact that very access itself, drew their attention away from each other and made their embrace a pose, so that even if their audience was only hypothetical, even it was only a later (by a minute or an hour, a year or many years) version of themselves, still it made their grappling, however passionate, performance.

Here Mitko, the Mitko who sat next to me, taking long draughts from the tumbler which he had refilled, put his finger on the screen, a finger stained with cigarettes (*mrusen*) and flattened with labor, broad and inelegant, the new wounds still fresh at the knuckle. Julien, he said, the man's name, and told me that he was his first *priyatel*,

using the word now in a way that was clear, his
first boyfriend and, he went on to tell me, his first
love. There were more pictures, always the two of
them alone, one or the other awkwardly angling
the camera. They were so young, these boys in
the frame, children really, and yet despite their
eagerness for each other it was as though in these
documents they gathered they acknowledged the
transience of things, even or especially of those
we hope most to hang on to; and recognized too
that the only memorials to what had passed would
be those they made, since of course there were no
witnesses in their little town to what they were
together, neither their families nor their friends,
not even the memories of anonymous witnesses
passed by on the street (none of the photos was
taken outside, in none was there a single witness).
Except for these photographs, then, these digital
memories he scrolled through now, nothing would
have survived of these embraces that for all their
heat passed in a moment, like so many things
leaving no trace. Where is he now, I asked Mitko,
still flooded with tenderness and wanting access to
some greater intimacy with him. He didn't look
at me as he answered, still clicking from image to
image, his hand moving absently across his bare
chest. He was a schoolteacher, Mitko told me, he
had gone to school abroad and lived in France,
having fled his country along with, it sometimes
seems, nearly everyone with the talent or means
to do so. Of these two men, then, locked together

indissolubly on the screen, one left, buoyed by talent or means or both, they do sometimes occur together; and the other stayed and was transformed somehow from the prosperous boy of that couple to the more or less homeless man I had invited into my home. How can we account for them, time and chance that together strip us of our promise, making of our lives almost always less than we imagined or was imagined for us, not maliciously or with any other intent, but simply because the measure of the world's solicitude is small?

But I wasn't thinking any of this then, not explicitly; I simply felt an overwhelming sorrow for him, unequivocally sorrow now, which swamped the desire that had been mounting for hours. As if he sensed this sadness and shared it and wanted to give it voice, Mitko opened a new page, a Bulgarian site where video clips are posted, a site where one can find almost anything, copyright laws having little meaning here. Music, Mitko said, I want you to hear something, and he typed the name of a French singer, someone I had never heard of and whose name escapes me now, into the little search engine that dredged up, from its digital memory, a remarkable number of files. Mitko scanned several pages, searching for the clip of a song he had shared with Julien, something they had listened to and loved together. Each of the little thumbnail images showed a frail woman softly lit, holding a microphone prayerfully in both of her hands. Perhaps all of these clips were from the same concert, or perhaps the simple, floor-length white gown she wore in each of them was a kind of signature. I was at first quite moved, as Mitko found the video he wanted and set it playing, feeling that he was granting me access to a private history and thus to the kind of intimacy I longed for with him; and that this music, so intricate with his past, might be the medium allowing this intimacy passage across our two languages. And yet, as I watched this woman, beautiful with a hollow sort of beauty, I found myself increasingly repelled by what seemed to me a transparent and entirely artless manipulation. She sang in a choked whisper, affecting an extremity of dignified, photogenic devastation, and at the end of a particularly tragic passage, without losing any of her composure she broke into tears, lowering the microphone in a posture of defeat. At several points the camera (it was a professional film, an elaborate concert video) had positioned itself as if at the singer's shoulder, forcing us into greater sympathy with her as we shared her vantage on the thousands of fans by which she was besieged, their mass stretching into the darkness. It was these thousands that burst into a kind of ecstasy at the sight of these tears, producing collectively a sound of mingled dismay and joy, having been provoked by this frail form to an intensity of emotion that seemed to carry with it its own warrant of authenticity, its own promise of the real. Ah, said that sound, here at last is the life of significance, the real life that frees us from ourselves. It wasn't the manipulation, which of course is the aim of all art, that offended me, but rather its bareness, the vulgarity of its methods, so that the whole apparatus of provocation and response lay stripped to its essential meanness.

These thoughts, which inserted greater and greater distance between myself and the moment I shared with Mitko, seemed also to reflect upon the emotions I had been made to feel (it came increasingly to seem) that very evening by Mitko himself. I felt, as I sat there enduring this wretched music, that I had been played as surely as this audience (if with greater skill), lured into a sentimentality entirely inappropriate to what was, after all, merely a transaction, anything else it might seem simply my own fantasy. This roused me, and even as Mitko continued looking tenderly at the screen, a look that now I suspected was artificial, calculated and sly (and perhaps I was right), I stood up, I put my hands on his shoulders and bent my face to his neck. *Haide*, I said, come on, tasting him and tugging at his shoulders. He tried at first to put me off, saying that we had time, that the night was long; he was counting on a place to spend that night, and no doubt had experience with hospitalities withdrawn in post-coital shifts of mood, with men whose desire dissolved immediately to disgust, as happens so often, our pleasures come so seldom unaccompanied by shame. But I insisted, wanting to assert something, to set the terms of the evening, to claim, finally, the goods for which I had contracted, to put it as brutally as that; it was something brutal that I wanted. When he saw I wouldn't be put off, Mitko turned compliant, even eager; he rose from the chair and put his arms around my neck, then hopped and wrapped his legs around me. I had never felt his weight before, I realized, all of our encounters having been to that point vertical, and I was surprised by his lightness as I carried him from the kitchen to the bed. The new sternness I had put on fell away from me there, it was I who was compliant, this compliance being, finally, what I had purchased. He was attentive and demanding by turns, practiced and sure and even inventive in the greater leisure and space we enjoyed. In sex he combined the same playfulness and brutality, the severe tenderness that was so distinctive in his person, and it was here, in bed, that I took his hands in mine, as I had imagined doing, his wounded hands, and brought them (perhaps to his bemusement) to my lips; and then I placed my own hands around him, lowering my face to him, clasping his hips like the brim of a cup from which I drank. He was wrong to have feared (if he did fear it) that my desire for his presence would disappear once he had settled our accounts, as it were, that I would ask him to return to the center and wander its streets. I wanted him to stay, even post-coitally I wanted to be intimate with him, to touch him without passion now but more tenderly, and it was with disappointment and even pain that I realized our contract didn't extend so far, that instead he was eager to break from our intimacy, bounding up off the bed. Everything good? he asked, *vsichko li e nared?*, reminding me (I was so eager now to forget it) that those acts in which we had engaged, however authentic or passionate they had seemed, partook of no other code save commerce, that any meaning or affect I ascribed to them was mine alone.

He receded down the hall naked, returning to the computer as I drew back on my clothes. I heard the sound of more gin being poured, then the pressing of keys, then the distinctive inflating chime of Skype opening. I returned to the room, fully clothed, and watched as Mitko began what would be a long series of conversations over the internet, voice and video chats with a number of other young men. I sat in a chair some distance behind him, where I could see the screen without myself falling within the frame. These men seemed all to be speaking from darkened rooms, in voices that were hushed, I realized gradually, to avoid disturbing their families sleeping (it was quite late now, one or two in the morning) in the next room. Many of them existed only as faces, all that could be seen of them in a single bulb's little circle of light. They greeted Mitko fondly, familiarly, though I would come to learn that he had never met most of them in the flesh, that the extent of their relations was restricted to these disembodied encounters. As I listened to these men, all of whom lived outside of Sofia, many of them in small villages and towns where they would have little opportunity for the exercise of their lives, I was struck by the strangeness of this community they had formed, at once so partial and so lively. Mitko moved from conversation to conversation, speaking and typing at once, the screen lighting up regularly with new invitations. I found myself lapsing into dullness, able to understand so little and increasingly submerged in exhaustion. Every now and again I would snap to attention, alerted by some stray word or tone of voice that Mitko was discussing me; and I felt a peculiar sense of helplessness on finding myself the object of conversations I couldn't understand or partake in. On one or two occasions Mitko even orchestrated a sort of introduction, tilting the little screen toward me so that I was captured in the image, and the stranger and I would smile awkwardly and wave at each other, having nothing at all to say. There was no reason I should have felt increasingly such a sense of shame as the night wore on, or that more and more I should suspect that I was the object of mockery or scorn; no reason besides, I suppose, the bitterness and simple jealousy I felt at my exclusion from Mitko's enthusiasm, the attention he lavished on these other men. To nourish or stave off this bitterness, I'm not sure which, or perhaps out of simple boredom, at some point I pulled from my shelf a volume of poems that I held open on my lap. It was a slim volume, Cavafy, which I chose I suppose in the hope that I would find in it some narrative to redeem my evening, to gild at least what

I felt increasingly to be the sordidness of it. But I was too exhausted to read and flipped the pages idly, afraid that if I went to bed I would wake up robbed, my apartment stripped of those toys that gave Mitko such delight, that he coveted and envied and that I neglected and (no doubt he felt) failed to deserve. As I looked at these pages, failing to find what I had gone to them for, I became gradually aware that the tenor of Mitko's conversations had changed, that he was no longer speaking fondly but suggestively, avariciously, and that his *priyateli* were now men older than he, men in their late thirties or forties. From stray words I caught it became clear that they were discussing preferences and scenarios and prices, that Mitko was arranging his week.

There was one man, older than the others, with whom the conversation was more prolonged. He was heavy-set and balding, with gray stubble on his face, a face that looked somehow at once both flabby and drawn in the flat light of the room where he sat smoking one cigarette after another. He lived in Plovdiv, Bulgaria's second city, which escaped bombing in WWII and thus has retained its beautiful center. As I listened to them speak to each other, listening not to their words but to the tones and cadences of their speech, I remembered the first time I visited this city, the first place I had been outside of Sofia and so my first acquaintance with the architecture typical of the National Revival, with its elaborate wooden structures and bright pastels, which should curdle beneath their own garishness but instead seem expressions of an irrepressible joy. Plovdiv was built, like Rome, as a city of seven hills, and Bulgarians sometimes still refer to it as such, though one of the hills was destroyed and mined, in communist times, for the stones that now pave the streets in the pedestrian center. On one of the remaining hills stands another mark of those times, a huge statue of a Soviet soldier, Alyosha he's called by the locals, around whom a large park descends the hill, at each level opening into plazas and observatory points with sweeping vistas of the city. One side of this park is maintained, with wide staircases and well-kempt paths, frequented by couples and families and weekend athletes, society in all its propriety parading its public life. On my first visit, however, I and a friend out of ignorance made our way up the other side of the hill, which had largely been left to its own devices and the acedia of rot. This side too had its stairways and plazas, though the stones seemed to crumble beneath us as we made our way, frequently grabbing at branches or shrubs for balance or even dropping to our hands and knees. And yet, as we climbed, it became clear that these paths had not been entirely deserted. At one point, pausing for a moment to look out at the city and back at the way we had come, we noticed a man on one of the lower observatories, a man we hadn't seen as we came up, either because he had hidden himself or because we were engrossed in our own exertions. We were struck by this man's strange actions, which we could interpret only after some time. He held a plastic bag in one of his hands, which now and again he would bring to his face, burying his mouth and nose in it and taking huge, famished breaths; even from our distance we could see the heaving of his shoulders, which shook as if he were weeping. As he lowered the bag from his face there was a kind of softening in his posture, a sinking or relaxing of his frame and an unsteadiness on his feet; and then he would straighten suddenly, and advancing to the rusted rail thrust out his arms toward the city, an expression of longing or ecstasy or grief that haunts me still. At one point he gripped this railing in both hands and leaned over it, neatly and with great composure vomiting into the bushes below. Increasingly, as we climbed, we came across strange abandoned structures, squat and concrete, slowly being dismantled by incursions of branches and roots, so that often only the bare outline of a room remained, sometimes only a single wall. At one observatory point, however, where again we stopped to catch our breath, there was a line of these structures, concrete shells that, though they lacked both doors and windows, seemed otherwise more or less intact. The interiors were opaque with shadow, and yet I had the impression that they extended back some distance, perhaps even burrowing into the rock, a network of little cells like a hive or a mine. From the rubbish which, so far as I could see, they were filled with, it was clear that they still had their uses, and as we stood there I became aware of the presence of three men standing not far away, men who had obscured themselves at our approach and now, as we hadn't immediately passed on, emerged from the shadows. They were solitary figures, all older and lean, each sheltering a cigarette in a cupped palm. Though they never acknowledged our presence or looked our way the air buzzed with an electric charge, and I knew that with a gesture I might retreat with one of them into those little rooms, as surely I would have (I was myself humming with it) had I not been with my friend, who was oblivious to anything save a vague unease.

Perhaps it was something reminiscent of this charge that caught my attention in this friend or client of Mitko's, a note of need I hadn't heard in the other men he had spoken with, a note I recognized. He seemed so eager to please, his eagerness mixed with trepidation and even dread; and it seemed to me that Mitko enjoyed the power he wielded, his power to be pleased or to withhold his pleasure. I have something for you, I heard this man say, and heard also *podaruk*, the word Mitko loved and that the man applied now to a cellular phone he held up to the camera, still in its box, one of the models Mitko had looked at so covetously on Graf Ignatief. And Mitko allowed himself to be pleased, he smiled at the man and thanked him, going so far even as to call his gift *strahoten*, a word that means awesome and is, like our word, built from a root signifying dread. You have to come get it, the man said, and

Mitko agreed, he would take a bus to Plovdiv the next day. As I sat there in my fatigue, realizing it was my money that would buy Mitko's ticket to this man and his expensive gift, I wondered how it was I had become one of these men in the dark, offering whatever was asked to rent something we wouldn't be given freely, accepting without complaint our own diminishment. And again I felt something rise in me, in dismay or revolt, something that insisted, still, on one's exceptionality, that refused to dissolve to one of those spot-lit finally faceless faces on the screen. But whatever it was that rose felt distant now, my resistance had weakened, whether through realism or fatigue; or perhaps it was simply that, having ridden this wave already so many times that evening, I knew it would ebb. Mitko had already introduced me to this man, he had tilted the screen toward me so that we could greet each other, which we did tentatively and with a shade of hostility on the other man's part, perhaps because I was younger than he and (for a little while yet) more attractive, because I had still some purchase on the youth that had so decidedly fled him, though less with each day, I see it feelingly; and perhaps simply because I still had tenure of Mitko, the man because of whom we stared at each other now as Mitko told him to hold up his *podaruk* again, for my admiration or, more likely, for my instruction. Mitko was still mine for the night, and although the night was itself already fleeing there were still hours in which he was mine to do with as I wished,

at least within the unwritten terms of our phantom
contract; hours in which I might deplete the desire
this man was counting on as his own, his reward
for the extravagance of his gift. It gave me some
pleasure to think of that depletion, feeling as I
did something of the jealousy of ownership, even
though my ownership was temporary, wasn't really
ownership at all, and even though I already felt the
bitterness of sending Mitko off the next morning
to Plovdiv and this other man, who had lured him
away so easily.

My fatigue had become a kind of agitation
now, I felt antsy, on edge, opening and closing the
book still lying unread on my lap. I hadn't found
in it what I wanted, as I say, what I had found in
it before, the recovery of something like nobility
from the mawkishness and shame of desire, the
sense that sex, even the most usually devalued—
stray meetings in dark rooms or the shadowy
commerce of my own evening—burned with
genuine luminosity, rubbing up against the realm
of the ideal, ready at the slightest provocation to be
transfigured, to become, as sex is always wont to do,
metaphysics. I set the book aside now, seeing that
Mitko was tired too, tired and noticeably drunk,
having emptied nearly two thirds of the bottle we
had bought, what seemed to me an astonishing
amount. He was unsteady on his feet when he stood
up, having said goodbye to the man in Plovdiv and
having announced his intention, finally, to sleep.
There were three hours left until we would have

to wake, he for his short trip to Plovdiv, a couple
of hours on a comfortable bus; and I for my day
of teaching, when I would stand before class after
class speaking as someone very different from who
I had been these hours, wearing a face scrubbed of
the eagerness and servility and need of the face I
wore as I followed Mitko to the bathroom, standing
behind him (he was still naked) as he stood to piss.
I ran my hands across his chest and stomach, lean
and taut, the skin of my hands catching just slightly
on the bristles of hair returning, it had been two or
three days since he had shaved; and then, at his
words of permission or encouragement, something
like Go on, I don't mind, my hands went lower
still, and gingerly I took the base of his cock in
my fingers and wrapped my hand around the shaft,
feeling beneath my fingers the flow of water, heavy
still and urgent, and feeling too my own urgency,
the hardness I pressed against him. He leaned his
head back then, pressing his face against mine,
rubbing it (it too was stubbled and rough) against
the softness of my own, and I felt him harden
as he finished pissing, as I carefully skinned him
back and shook the last of it, feeling myself almost
suffocated with longing, with longing and fatigue,
having never touched anyone so intimately, having
never been before of that particular service. Mitko
turned to me now, he pressed himself to me and
kissed me, deeply and searchingly and possessingly,
at the same time pushing me backwards down the
hallway toward the bedroom, pushing me and

perhaps also using me as a support, to the broad bed where we had lain together earlier and where now we lay down again, not for sex now but to sleep, exhausted despite our arousal. I felt that arousal again as Mitko turned toward me and embraced me, wrapping his arms around me and pulling me close to him, and not just his arms, he wrapped his legs around me too and with all four of his limbs pressed me to him, an active exertion, embracing me so that when I breathed in the air was filtered through him, smelling of alcohol of course but also of his own scent that elicited such an animal response from me, that so fired me up (I imagined the chambers of the brain lighting up, thrown switches in a house). And it was as animals that we slept, he like some marine creature wrapped about me, wrapping about me again if I shifted or half-woke, and I held like <u>his cherished thing</u> or his child, sleeping as I have seldom slept, deeply and almost without disturbance; or held, I suppose it must be said, like <u>his conquest</u> or his prey.

THERE'S A POROUSNESS TO THESE PAGES, WHICH are written with a kind of fickleness or fecklessness, so that what happens in the present (in my current present, now, before it becomes a more vivid and significant past) as I think these retrospective thoughts can enter, pervade and shift the currents of retrospection. But it's also true that these pages, which accrue so slowly and with such effort, change in their turn the reception of the present, digging channels which determine how new experiences are processed and perceived. Not long ago, for instance, I found myself in Blagoevgrad, in the Pirin mountains, escorting a group of students to a conference on mathematical linguistics, a field in which I have little interest and no expertise. I had long hours, while they were in lectures, to explore the beautiful wooded park near our hotel, which followed a small river three kilometers or so toward the pedestrian city center, a haven of humane architecture almost untouched by the ravages of Soviet-era construction, though blemished here and there by gaudy new buildings, expensive apartments overlooking the river. It was spring, early yet, the *asmi* were still bare, the wooden trellises built over benches and tables for grape vines to climb, vines which now were still withered and dry; there was no sign on them yet of their shade-giving foliage, much less of their fruit. They clung to their wooden supports, vestiges of winter in a landscape already lush with the turned year. The trees were bright with fresh leaves and already obscene with flowers, flowers of a sort I had never seen before, extravagant and eager blossoms and buds and cones of flowers, a kind of elaborate drunkenness. Our hotel was at the edge of the town, where human habitation made a half-hearted charge further up the mountains, getting nowhere, so that past the hotel's vigorously mowed and always encroached upon lawn there was sheer wildness, impenetrable woods and thickets and, just a little further up, dramatic crags. Even in the park along the river, where I spent my mornings, there was a kind of romantic wildness to the path between the great shorn face of the mountain and the river, which, though small, charged from the peaks with remarkable speed, roaring as it beat against rocks already broken in its bed. Walking along that path, wondering at the profusion around me, I felt drawn from myself, elated, entirely engrossed and set free, struck somehow stupidly good for a moment at the extravagant beauty of the world. The air was thick with movement, butterflies and day-moths and also, hanging iridescent in the sun, the tiny ephemerae shining and embalmed, pushed here and there by the light breeze, against the pressure of which they had no recourse, as against the pressure of that other element, time, which bears against us all and to which all of us give way. But the air bore also its inadequate answer to time, the grasses and trees having released in a great exhalation pods of seeds, the little generative grains each sheltered and propelled by a tuft of hair like a parachute or umbrella; they swarmed in my clothes and hair, as in the clothes and hair of everyone walking there, all of us feeling the same elation. I thought, as I stood watching this sowing of the earth, of Whitman, whose poems I had just been teaching to the students now flickering between boredom and interest as they listened to their lectures on mathematical linguistics, lectures they would recount to me over dinner in the little town, telling me also how they imagined my reaction to the arguments made about poetry and the structures of meter and rhyme, their numerical claims on our pleasure. Standing in that path, feeling on my skin the procreant threads seeking purchase, catching on my clothes to be carried who knows where, to what fertile or what barren ground, I thought of lines that had always seemed overreaching to me, audacious and enthusiastic, a source of minor embarrassment on my part and of joy to my students, of delighted laughter, lines in which the whole world stands

46

sharpened to an erotic point, aimed at the poet lain bare before it. They had always mildly embarrassed me, as I say, and yet it was these lines that came to me on the path in Blagoevgrad watching seeds come down like snow, that determined and defined and enriched that moment, language as always interposing itself between ourselves and what we see. What were they, these seeds, if not the wind's soft-tickling genitals, the world's procreant urge; and finally it felt plausible to me, his desire to be bare before that urge, his madness, as he says, to be in contact with it. I felt something of that desire myself, though it was nothing like madness for me in my life pitched almost always beneath the pitch of poetry, a life of inhibition and perhaps missed chances and experiences, but also a bearable life, a life that to some extent I had chosen and continued to choose.

After crossing a little wooden footbridge, at the middle of which I stopped for a moment, peering at the churning waters and feeling their vibration in the structure that held me above them, I found a small café nestled in a bend in the river, on a plot of land the waters had spared. The café was a small structure, little more than a shack, but modern and well kept; the seating consisted of picnic tables arranged haphazardly by the water. Many of these were taken already, and I had to sit back from the river, though still well within the reach of the sound of it, that sound that has always, since my earliest childhood, soothed me and eased somewhat the anxieties and uncertainties and ceaseless churnings of the brain that have at times so overwhelmed and almost, as it seems, crippled me. From my table I could watch, as I sipped my cup of coffee and warm milk, the other tables, many of them taken by large groups about which there was a certain festivity, so that I remembered there was indeed a festival of some sort that day or weekend, there are too many here to keep track. Children were playing by the water, in pairs and groups, with balls and sticks and plastic guns emitting light and sound. As I watched them, ignoring the papers I had brought with me to review, my attention was caught by a younger child standing separate from the rest, perhaps three or four years old and kept company by a man I took to be her father. They were stationed at the very edge of the water, the girl standing and the man crouching behind her. Repeatedly, as I watched, this girl, anchored at the waist by the arm of the man behind her, leaned perilously forward (though there was no peril) over the sharp bank, looking down at the water rushing two or three feet beneath her. Repeatedly she leaned forward and repeatedly sprang back, returning to stability and certainty with delighted laughter. On the fourth or fifth repetition of this game, the child leaned out even farther than before, so far that the man had to extend his anchoring arm away from his body, almost as far as it would reach. She didn't laugh upon return this time, as if shocked and perhaps unnerved by her own audacity, the risk she took in leaning out so far, which of course wasn't a risk at all with her father's arm around her, permitting no incursion of doubt; instead of laughing, she thrust herself back against her father's body and, throwing her arms up to clasp his neck, pulled his head down (or perhaps she didn't have to pull it down), embracing it close to her own. Only then did she laugh, with her father's body folded around her; she laughed with a kind of joy it was difficult for me to recognize, so certain it seemed of a home among the things of the world. They embraced each other for a long time, a kind of physical contact seldom seen in public, maybe seen only between parents and their very young children, an intimacy free of the anxieties or urgencies of sex and confident of absolute possession. Perhaps here, I thought to myself, was a wholly untheatrical embrace. One could recognize it as a beautiful thing, even as one felt a certain melancholy of exclusion, and even as I reflected on the process by which, so soon and (it seemed to me) with such grief that intimacy would be rendered illegitimate, as the child grew older and began (entirely without intention or choice) to respond differently to these embraces, these touches and caresses, so that the same touch that here warmed our hearts (I was not the only one touched, others watched as well, smiling and wistful, envious perhaps of one of the parties or perhaps of both) would in just a year or two elicit our disapproval, our concern or even our scorn. And so it is, I thought then, as the man and his child released each other and retreated from the water and as I prepared finally to bend my head to my work, so it is that at the very moment we come into full consciousness of ourselves and begin gathering impressions with which to stock that consciousness, developing thereby the habitudes and expectations that will form the personalities we are graced or burdened by, at this very moment what we experience is leave-taking and loss, a pang and a wound that is then inextricable from who we are, a betrayal (if it is a betrayal) the size and the shape of which determine the size and the shape of what we ourselves become. Or perhaps it isn't like this at all; perhaps all I sketched out for myself, silently and with mingled bitterness and longing as I watched the man and his child return to their table to (I presumed) the child's mother and grandparents, who welcomed her too with embraces, perhaps all of this is (like so much else) mere fantasy and etiological myth, fantasy and myth having always been our preferred means of excavating the depths of ourselves and seeking out the sources of our discontent. For a moment, at least, it seemed plausible to me, the story I told about the sense of dislocation I so often feel and the pang that was eased for the few hours I slept embraced by Mitko, the embrace I returned to in my thoughts (as I have so often) as I watched the child and her father by the river in Blagoevgrad.

It had already been, by that morning I spent marking papers, more than two months since my final meeting with Mitko in Varna, a meeting that itself was preceded by three months of strange silence, silence I demanded (as I thought) some weeks after the night we spent together in my apartment in Mladost, one of only two nights, as it turned out, we would spend together in the several months of our acquaintance. In the days and weeks that followed that night, Mitko appeared at my apartment repeatedly and unannounced, always friendly and eager, and always with some request. I came to dread these requests, not for their exorbitance (they were never that), but because they stripped to such bareness the mechanism of our relations, the brevity of the ensuing encounters unaccommodating of significance or of the metaphysical fantasy I so longed for. Hearing the ringing in my apartment of the bell linked to the street entrance, which no one else ever rang, I found myself torn between a desire on the one hand for the routines of solitude (my writing and my books), with the release they offer from the doubts and divinations, the endless calculations that attend for me any society at all, however desired; and, on the other, for the thrill of Mitko's presence, with its disruption of routine and its nonliterary pleasures. It was, as I say, after weeks of these visits that I felt I needed to free myself of them, although I still found, as on this occasion, that my heart leapt up at the little buzzer's announcement of his presence. Though he wore his usual expression of eager amiability and seemed well enough, I was

concerned at the state of him, and particularly
at the sour smell rising off him, of clothes worn
several days without washing. We had just installed
ourselves on the couch, he had just smiled at me in
invitation and I had just laid my head on his chest,
enduring the sour smell which anyway didn't bother
me terribly, when the buzzer rang a second time. I
felt both relief and annoyance at being reminded of
the dinner I had forgotten, my friend C., another
teacher at the College, having come to collect me
and to walk the short distance to the restaurant
we frequented. Mitko was delighted to see this
friend, whom he had met before and by whom he
was clearly smitten, as was nearly everyone who
met C., who had a kind of effortless, ingratiating
charm and was nonetheless entirely indifferent to
the needs and desires of others, so that he seemed
always to be receding from one while still inviting
pursuit. Mitko hardly took his eyes off of him and
touched him whenever he could, always robust
and friendly touches, a kind of physical language
to compensate for their inability to speak to each
other; and yet touches that, though there was
nothing at all seductive about them, I knew would
at the slightest sign of permission or desire have
taken on a sexual heat. I was jealous of this interest
that Mitko showed, of course, which was different
in kind from the interest he showed for me, but
then I was in love with C. too, if with a love both
partial and unreturned.

At dinner, where Mitko ordered far more than

he could consume, food and drink and cigarettes, I was soon exhausted by my attempts to translate between them, and we settled quickly into a silence interrupted by Mitko's sallies at conversation, nearly all of them directed, through me, to C. It was perhaps out of jealousy, then, or perhaps out of some more benign motive that I suddenly asked Mitko whether he liked his life among his *priyateli*, putting the question as baldly as that. No, he answered with the same baldness, showing his usual reticence to discuss anything unpleasant, especially regarding the past or the strange paths by which he had reached his present. I pressed him, again unsure whether out of cruelty or interest or concern, and, entirely neglecting my friend, who was unable to follow even my own halting Bulgarian, I asked Mitko why he chose then to live as he did. I knew the question was naïve, or not even that, that in its terms it was unfair and presumed a freedom of action that served to prime a kind of judgment, a judgment I was the last person in the world to have any grounds to cast. But Mitko's answer was equally naïve: *Sudba* he said, fate, the single word serving to dismiss at a stroke all choice and consequence. In Varna there were no jobs, he said, and in Sofia the jobs there were were shut off to him, since he had no address he could give to employers, and no means of securing such an address without work. This was the end of our exchange, which changed the color of the evening, for the rest of which there would be no more innuendo from Mitko

(innuendo which I had received ambivalently, to
his visible confusion, accustomed as he was to my
need) and during which in other respects as well
his mood was subdued, as was my own, subdued
and also shifting, wanting at once to repair the
damage I had done and sensing with some relief the
possibility of extricating myself from a relation that
had come to seem more intricate than I could bear.
It seemed to me that there was no bearing toward
Mitko I could take that might allow me to feel at
once sufficiently compassionate and sufficiently
free, an ambivalence that, though exacerbated by
the special circumstances of my relation with him
and by his own mixture of the innocent and (as
it seemed to me) the sly, was nonetheless chronic,
a repeating movement of expansion and retreat
that characterized all of my relations, casual and
profound. But there was nothing sly in his mood as
we walked, the three of us, toward the Metro after
dinner, I having made clear that this once, at least,
there wouldn't be sex between us. I was relieved to
make this clear, to find I was capable of making it
clear, and yet still I didn't feel at ease with myself or
with him, all the more so when, in response to my
asking if he was all right, unable to bear anymore
his silence or his evident sadness, he said, *iskam da
zhiveya normalno*, I want to live a normal life. I felt
remorse at this, but also that my necessary escape
from it, from it and from Mitko himself, could
come only by pushing further, by telling him that
I didn't want to become one of his clients, waving

away his objection that he considered me a friend. I liked him too much, I said, clumsily but with candor, it isn't good for me to like you so much. We had reached the station by then, and he stood a moment looking at me with a sort of bemusement, not quite sure what to make of what I had said, or perhaps wondering, as I had so often, which of the faces I had shown him was the true face, the face of need that he had been accustomed to, of passion and of need, or this new face that suddenly was closed to him. Then, as if resigning himself to a bemusement it wasn't worth his while to resolve, he shrugged and put out his hand, asking for a ten leva note to see him on his way.

FOR THREE MONTHS THERE WAS NO SIGN OF MITKO, and over the course of that time my surprise that he would take seriously my final words to him turned gradually to concern and finally, inevitably, to longing. It was a weekend afternoon in February that with a little ping he appeared on Skype, from which he had been absent all that time, as he had been absent from NDK and from the streets I had begun only half aware to haunt in the hope of finding him again and of picking up the thread I had (as it seemed to me now) too quickly and with too little thought, too cavalierly let drop. How extraordinary that with a motion allowing no time for consideration or regret or the reflex of retreat, with the press of a key my screen should suddenly be filled with the moving image of him, undeniable, dear to me again after the long absence. He was peering at his own screen, his face at first knit with attention suddenly relaxing and coming alive, smiling with what seemed a genuine smile at seeing me, as it were, after all this time. As we spoke, a little shyly at first, I did little but look at him; for the hour or so that we stayed on each other's screens I stared at his image as if to consume it, taking in at long draughts what I was surprised to find I had nearly forgotten: not the still details, which I could consume at leisure in the photographs I had taken of him, of his every inch as he modeled for me the long night he spent in my apartment; not the still details but the enlivened whole, the million movements he made that were the living tale of him and that filled me, as I watched him, with happiness and also with a longing stripped of all ambivalence. He looked the same, absolutely the same, and it was a shock to learn that almost the entire time of our separation, some ten of the twelve or thirteen weeks of his disappearance, he had been in a hospital in Varna, laid up with a liver disorder, though I couldn't make out the details, either because of my Bulgarian or because he shied away from revelation. As usual, he seemed not to want to dwell on an unpleasant past, but he did speak of the terrible boredom of the hospital, where he was forced to leave off his ceaseless movement, without a computer or even a television, as the one mounted in his room would only play if fed constantly with coins. Nor were books or even magazines a diversion, since he read Cyrillic with difficulty; having left school in the seventh grade, he was more comfortable with the Latin characters used in the internet chat rooms he frequented. He confessed this to me with evident shame one day when I had run out briefly for something he wanted—cigarettes or alcohol or the sweets he adored—and returned to find him at the computer moaning with frustration, unable *stuck between* either to type in the Cyrillic script it was set to or to switch it back.

He spent the long days and nights, then, in boredom and often in pain, visited on occasion by his mother and grandmother and (I supposed) the boy he called *brat mi* whom I hadn't seen since that first day in NDK. But he was better now, he said, he felt fine, though he expected to return to the hospital in a few weeks or a month, for a stay that was likely to be as long as the first. I thought of how often, for all his ebullience, I had seen Mitko sick, his colds and the ear infection he had had for months, the herpes that sometimes disfigured his mouth; I thought of the heaviness of his drinking and of course of the risks of his trade, and again I felt the desire simply to rescue him, though from what exactly and by what means I wasn't sure. I realized the futility and even the danger *Privilege* of this desire, and realized too that Mitko had never expressed any desire of his own to be saved. Of another kind of desire, however, he was well-stocked, and as our virtual encounter continued he made use more and more often of the keyboard, writing comments too salacious for the internet café he was writing me from. This had its effect, the effect he intended, overwhelmingly when he stood and under the pretext of stretching displayed his body to me, reaching into his pockets to pull the folds of his jeans tight against his crotch. By the end of the conversation, surprising myself, I had proposed to come to Varna at the end of the week, a proposition he was eager to accept. I will be with you the whole weekend, he said, I promise, *hundert protzent.*

Over the next few days I received a number of emails from him, each canceling the last as he visited hotels, reporting on prices and conveniences and their nearness to the sea. It was the sea, as the days passed in mounting anticipation, that I longed for almost as much as I longed for Mitko, having spent so many months in landlocked Sofia, and it was the thought of the sea even more than of Mitko that I dwelled on for the seven cramped hours I spent on the bus from Sofia to the coast. It was a gray day, cold, belonging more to winter than to the incipient spring, the only signs of which were the little bundles of red and white yarn everyone wore pinned somewhere to their clothes, remnants of the first of March ritual celebrated here to encourage the year to turn. My own bag was covered with these little charms, students having given them with great ceremony, with wishes of health and wealth and happiness, all that day. But whatever magic inhered in them had yet to act, and the entirety of the trip there fell a light cold rain that repeatedly edged to snow. I found myself despite my excitement depressed by both

the weather and the landscape we passed, which
seemed everywhere human hands had touched it to
have been irremediably marred. Along the highway,
which surely itself dated to communist times, the
habitations we passed were invariably squat and
concrete and often falling apart, abandoned no
doubt for their larger counterparts in the city I had
just left. I became increasingly amazed, pressing my
face to the large window, by how entirely it seemed
the impulse to beauty had been erased from these
utilitarian dwellings, so different, in everything
but their poverty, from the mountain villages I
had visited, places where every dwelling however
meager showed as if defiantly the urge toward art.

Never having been able to read on buses, I
found that the only other occupation available to
me was watching the little screens running the
length of the center aisle, three or four of them
all showing the same terrible American action
movie, a cheap pageant of the basest and most
satisfying passions, of injury and revenge and a
hero's triumph in blood. Eventually, as the world
darkened and was lost to me, I found myself with
no choice but to watch this film, which repeated
three times over the course of the trip and in which
I was immediately engrossed, despite the lack of
sound and the subtitles that moved too quickly
for me to puzzle them out. But really nothing was
needed beyond the broad language of the images
themselves, which showed a man stripped by
human malevolence of any civilizing influence,

reduced to misery and calculating rage, the orgiastic indulgence of which would be the chief source of our entertainment. And we were entertained, all of us (nearly everyone on the bus) watching the film, we felt together this man's griefs and rage, we shared with him and with each other a desire for blood and shared too an almost unbearable tension until that blood was spilled. It was only after the film was over, with its explosions and gunfire and far less mundane miseries, its elaborately baroque tortures, that I marveled at the cheap mastery of it, this engrossment and strumming of the passions, the narcotic exhilaration of certitude, and marveled too at my own responsiveness, the ease with which I was stoked to the heights of emotion, the far extremities of response, by the least nuanced fiction. How easily we are made to feel, I thought, and with what little foundation, with no foundation at all. And how facile, I thought then, as I had thought repeatedly while watching the extravagant Hollywood films I adore, films far more sophisticated than the movie I had just watched, which had never seen the inside of a theater but had instead gone directly to video and to captive audiences traveling on Balkan bus lines, films more sophisticated but no less crude in the emotions they provoked and exercised and trained—how facile any argument that claims the moral neutrality of art, of these narratives that teach us to feel, that take us from the depths to the heights and make any middle realm irrelevant, intolerable in its irrelevance.

But these thoughts were forgotten as we neared Varna, the lights of which (as had the lights of Veliko Turnavo, of Shumen) drew me back to the windows, to the blurred world glimpsed through glass streaked with rain. We stopped on the edge of the city center, or what I took to be the city center, not at a terminal but in a lot beside a gas station, where Mitko was standing without a hat or umbrella, his shoulders hunched against the rain. I was first off the bus, bounding off it to greet him, so overcome with excitement that he had to send me back for my bag, which I had left on the seat beside me. We both laughed at this, at my eagerness and forgetfulness, and he shook his head in what seemed to me affectionate rebuke, rebuke and indulgence, having done me again a service at once indispensable and beyond the terms of our contract. He continued this service, taking my bag with a kind of gallantry and leading me to a line of taxis, asking me about the trip, if I was hungry, if I wanted to go straight to the hotel or instead to explore a bit, though of course he already knew my answer to these questions. We arrived after a short time at the hotel he had chosen for us, where I had called earlier in the week to make our reservation, a nice place, he had said, very close to the sea. And it was nice, in a declining sort of way, two old houses around a courtyard on a little side street off the city's main square, the pedestrian avenue leading to the sea. There was a single attendant, an old man who came out of his little booth, a glassed-in porch

attached to one of the buildings, to greet us. He
and Mitko shook hands warmly, and I wondered
to myself what their relationship was, whether
Mitko came here often with men, whether perhaps
they had some arrangement. Our room was shabby
and large, on the first floor with windows facing
the street, large bay windows fastened with a little
latch and inadequate against the wind. There was
a stand-alone radiator against one of the walls, and
Mitko immediately went to it; he must have been
chilled to the bone from his wait. He sat on the
radiator, having switched it on, and visibly relaxed
with pleasure as it warmed. Without getting up, he
reached to the old television against one of the walls
of the room and flipped through the few channels,
stopping at a station playing videos of Balkan pop-
folk songs; he hummed along, wagging his head
from side to side with the jagged rhythms as he
fiddled with my iPod, which I had set down on
arriving and which he had immediately snatched
up. It took him a moment to realize that it wasn't
the same device that had so fascinated him in Sofia.
When I told him that it had been stolen, that a
man had taken it from me during an encounter, he
shook his head in sympathy—such is the world—
and then his features hardened. When I'm in Sofia,
he said, we'll look for him, you show me who he is
and I'll take care of him. *Samo da go vidya i do tam.*
It was clear that his sickness, whatever it was, hadn't
kept him from the brawls he evidently enjoyed;
above his left eye, now, there was a wound just a

day or two old, the skin still split. I tried to occupy myself, in the face of his evident absorption, as best I could, settling in a bit, arranging my things, but my tension and my desire and my joy at seeing him were too much for me, I went to him and touched him and he put his hand on my neck and pushed me down, then unbuttoned his fly and fished himself out, never putting down the little contraption that so fascinated him. It was only after several minutes, when I stood up again and took his arm and tugged him toward the bed, that he laid the device aside and made himself more fully available to me. But he was still detached, giving the bulk of his attention to the television, and when I asked him what was wrong he just shrugged a little and answered that he had already had sex that afternoon, which seemed like a breach of contract although of course I had no real basis for complaint. I fell back from him then, I lay next to him thinking, as I had had cause to think before, of how helpless desire is outside its little theater of heat, how ridiculous it becomes the moment it isn't welcomed and reflected, even if that reflection is contrived. And also how lonely, with a kind of absolute isolation and exclusion, even as Mitko was right next to me, naked now and stretched out beside me with his arms behind his head, granting me an unrestricted access that did nothing to assuage my sense of the lack of him, even as it was his warmth next to me that I strove to feel as I brought myself off.

I woke early the next morning and walked out

into the little streets on my own. The sun was just rising, the air was chill and fresh and laced with salt, borne by the insistant wind. Mitko had said that the hotel was close to the sea, but there was no preparing, as I turned from our little street into the main plaza, for the horizon of water so suddenly and with such presentness before me, framed grandly by the pillars at the entrance of the Sea Garden. I quickly lost myself in this park, wandering paths that seemed to lead toward the water only to veer away, curving unpredictably and as if endlessly into the interior, which had its own fascinations, not least its silence and its seemingly endless resources for solitude, or rather the rhythm it established of solitude and conviviality, deserted paths giving out suddenly into a kind of clearing or square, with benches gathered at observatory points over the sea, which was endless and gray and pierced ceaselessly by gulls. I found myself unaccountably moved by this park, assuaged, I suppose, after the desolations of landscape I had passed the day before, to be in a place designed so clearly with the sole aim of beauty, the very layout of the paths, with their apparent goallessness, reprimanding the utility enthroned elsewhere as the only goal admissable in the accoutrement of human life. Or not quite its sole aim, since as I wandered the park, which was begun shortly after the liberation, it became clear how bound it was to the history of its country, with its statues of revolutionaries and writers, its monuments to the fallen, so that

art & morality again

walking it one walked too a strangely lyrical account of the past, moments and figures stumbled upon in no particular order, stripped of their usual narrative and triumph, and returned, it seemed to me, to the vague aimlessness of memory. And there were signs too of other uses, more secret and ludic, in the darkest and most overgrown eddies, cigarette butts and bottles and the occasional distended dry husk of a condom left surely from the previous year's season, when these paths would have been carnivalesque with thousands of young vacationers from across Europe, the beautiful young fueled by night and heat and the ever-present sea.

It was the sea that I longed for now, after so much delay and misdirection, the sea that was so close and yet seemingly inaccessible. Again and again the occasional staircases I encountered leading down from the garden's observatories to the beach were cordoned off, in such crumbling disrepair as to disallow safe passage. I was aware of time passing and felt myself drawn back to the hotel, to Mitko where perhaps he was waking to find me gone. I was frustrated again to find, when finally I made my way down from the Garden toward the beach, that access to the water was blocked by a seemingly endless line of construction, complexes of restaurants and casinos and discotheques and hotels, all of them boarded up for the off-season, barricaded against sea and weather and, I assumed, the plundering hands that had covered these boards with graffiti. And yet, when finally I did find a way through these linked complexes, reaching not quite the beach yet but the road running alongside it, I found myself turning, after only a few moments, from the water I had so longed for and that was so beautiful, the sound of which was now palpable, a thrumming through my whole body. I turned both because the wind coming off it was so fierce, unbroken now by trees or by the buildings that had frustrated my approach, and also because those buildings proved so fascinating in themselves, with elaborately themed facades whose garishness was mitigated by desolation. While I could hear a radio playing faintly from within one of the restaurants, there was no sign of human presence, no voices or movement save for the cats that had improvised some habitation on the rooftops, where they watched me, disinterested and alert. Indeed, for much of my walk I moved in the intensest solitude, a kind of ghostliness of disuse. Most of the storefronts, as I say, were boarded up, huge wooden planks stripping the glass fronts of their views, but there was one restaurant that didn't suffer or enjoy this protection, I don't know why, and I walked up the few steps to the deck to peer in through the glass, which was crusted with salt and sand. It was a place for children, a kind of combination restaurant and playground, with figurines and little coin-operated rides in the shapes of figures from American cartoons. These contraptions were themselves wrapped in sheets of plastic, further blurring an image already blurred

by the glass, so that they were somehow distorted
and estranged from their familiarity, their cheap
ubiquity and fame. I found myself disconcertingly
repulsed by them, as if by a sense of taboo or a fear
almost of contagion, as though they were victims of
some malediction or specimens of plague preserved
in jars. Perhaps it was because of the elaborateness
of this effort at conservation, applied as it was to
images I associated with childhood and braced so
desperately against the sea (which without malice
or intention will consume it all), that the very
desperation seemed to reflect upon these plastic
marvels a kind of agonized life, so that they seemed
like infants themselves, suffocating in plastic cauls.

Mitko was awake when I returned to the hotel,
lounging and watching television and unperturbed,
or so it seemed to me, by my absence, though he
wanted to know where I had been and took my
camera to scan through the photos I had taken. He
knew every inch of the park, he said, he recognized
each of the scenes framed on the little screen, and
he demonstrated this knowledge by describing for
me what the frame hadn't caught. It was with the
same expertise that he took me into the city that
afternoon, through its little streets and squares,
many of which seemed miniatures of those in the
capital I had left, as did its landmarks: monuments
to the same patriots, museums of history, of
archeology and ethnography, the Roman ruins
and the central cathedral, with its efflorescence of
domes. But these resemblances were as nothing to

the difference of the place, its quietness (despite the throb of the sea) and the salt twinge of the air. Everywhere there were gulls, tame and inquisitive as cats, filling the plazas and squares with their strange cries. Mitko was hungry, and so we stopped at a snack stand, a kind of bakery selling cheese pastries and sausages and sweets of various kinds. We stood in the street to eat, a little pedestrian square lined, as I remember, on one side by the opera house, and immediately we were accosted by one of these birds, who trotted intently before us, working the hinges of its bill and raising its wings as it barked out to us. Mitko had, as always, ordered more food than he could eat, and he tossed one of his scraps to this beggar, which beat its wings to catch it midair, tossing it back quickly and repeating its demands. Soon there were four or five of them stomping their feet and calling, calling, so that the air was full of opening doors. They delighted me, these creatures, and Mitko fed my delight as he fed the birds, to the last scrap, after which he raised his hands at once to confess and apologize for their poverty. As we continued our walk that day, increasingly Mitko gave me a sense of the city's private history, the intrication of its streets with his own intimacies: here the restaurant he frequented with Julien, here the scene of a nocturnal encounter, here the little table outside of a *dyuner* stand where, drunk and brawling, he struck his mouth and broke his tooth. When it was dark, he told me, he would take me to the thermal baths, pools where despite the cold we could lounge together. And he wanted me to see his home, he said; the next morning we would take the bus to the *blokove* ringing the city and I would meet his mother and his grandmother. I was surprised by this, I suppose I was something he wanted to show off to them, a foreigner, a teacher at a famous school, though how he would explain our acquaintance I had no idea.

He knew everyone, or so it seemed, at each corner or little shop greeting people by name, shaking their hands, patting their backs like a politician, an unaccountably public man. He gestured toward me in introduction, saying that I was his friend, an American, at which point I nodded politely and waited for the encounter to end. As we walked away, on more than one occasion Mitko leaned into me and whispered some man's availability, suggesting we might all three have fun together, he could easily arrange it, it would be a pleasure for all of us. But I wanted my pleasure to be with Mitko alone, and I told him this later, back in the room when he suggested he call his friend, the one he called *brat mi* who was, he assured me, as eager as Mitko himself for the three of us to meet. We would gather at the hotel, he said, and then go to the hot springs together. It was already early evening, night was falling, he suggested that we might leave soon. But I want to be with you, I said, only with you, and he smiled a little and allowed himself to be dragged to the bed, allowed me to tug off his shoes, to unbutton his pants and his shirt. He lay next to

client
boyfriend
friend —
same
word

me, accepting in a noncommittal way my caresses and attentions, but entirely detached, propping himself up to drink from the whisky he had poured himself as soon as we got in, from which he drank deeply despite his illness and his pledge, he had told me, to drink less. He was watching television as well, flipping through channels until he stopped at a film, an American film dubbed in Bulgarian, as though to distract himself from what I was doing to him, so that I felt myself not only cast again into the intense solitude of my own longing but also into a sense of myself as an aggressor, exploiting a consent that was either constrained or so passive as to be as if given only at some remove. I didn't know how to respond to this sense of things; I pulled back from him and he didn't object, instead reaching down and starting to stroke himself, slowly and with something like languor, without urgency and with seemingly little desire but not stopping, even as he faded in and out of hardness keeping the same slow motion of his arm.

It was now, lying next to him but excluded finally from this seemingly mechanical exercise, that I could notice the film he had chosen. It was a famous film, recent, an historical drama that for all its costumed distance was as brutal as the film I had watched the day before. But this was a different sort of violence, less inventive but more graphic, more invested in genuine suffering and in the intimacy of an earlier technology, so that it wasn't gunfire and explosions we watched, Mitko and I, but the lashing of whips and the hacking of swords, the unabstractions of blood and pain. It killed my desire, but Mitko watched it without once looking away, not avidly but with a strange dullness, the same quality with which his hand moved at his waist. Can we change it, I said, can we watch something else, but he murmured no, he was watching it, it was interesting and he wanted to see what would happen. It was a famous story to me, history I had learned in school, as a child and then again later when it was more available to me, more available and more horrible; I knew what would happen, and I didn't want to be drawn with it to the irredeemable griefs of history, that cumulative helplessness portrayed on the screen. It disturbed me, the juxtaposition of these scenes of desire and repulsion, and I wanted him to stop jerking off to these images, though it didn't seem to me that that was quite what he was doing, the two actions—his eyes motionless and his hand in constant motion—seemed detached, though they shared the same quality of languor. Maybe you want to stop, I said, you don't have to finish now, using the Bulgarian euphemism, *svurshish*, more accurate but less hopeful than our own verb, come, the strange openness of which I preferred, you can wait until later. But he didn't want to wait, he said he was close though he wasn't close, there was still no urgency in his movement, no variation of tempo, though (I thought to myself) there was a strange aimless athleticism to it, or at least

viewpoint & privilege

endurance, he must have been getting tired. So I lay there for another quarter hour, watching him and watching the images on the screen, images of atrocity and an image of desire, though I could feel no desire, could feel nothing but a strangely acidic sense of entrapment. It was with a certain eagerness and solace that I slid now into this sense that I had been myself if not quite victimized then at least maltreated, excluded from the pleasures I had come so far for and that were, in any case, already and repeatedly bought and paid for; excluded from those pleasures and subjected, instead, to this fairly grueling display, which so tore at and disturbed me. He did finally finish, and it was only then that he touched me, at the last moment reaching out and pulling my head to him and filling my mouth, which felt less like an erotic attention than an act of convenience, a way quite simply of cleaning up. And now his languor disappeared, he seemed pleased with himself, filled with an ebullient energy. The third time today, he said, turning to me and grinning as at some accomplishment, explaining, at my evident confusion, that he had brought himself off twice that morning, alone, while I was exploring the Sea Garden. What do you mean, I said, at first sincerely, though even as I spoke my surprise was changing to something else, so that a note in what I said, in the tone of it, put Mitko on his guard, a guard that at first took on its own semblance of confusion. What, he said, lifting himself from the bed to the chair beside it and reaching for the pack of cigarettes he had already emptied, so that he crumpled it in annoyance and tossed it aside. He reached instead for his drink, though it too was empty and he had to pour himself another from the bottle on the floor. Are you angry at me, he asked, and I wasn't quite, anger wasn't really what I felt myself coming into, or it wasn't the dominant note of a music that was so familiar to me that however faintly it began I knew already its conclusion, which filled me even now with a kind of dread. Why would you do that, I said, why would you do that alone when you know how much I want it, and I couldn't do any better than that, stripped of the eloquence that is my chief defense; I had to speak with a kind of bareness, a lack of strategy or recourse. But you weren't here, Mitko said, I woke up and you were gone, I didn't know where or when you would be back, why should I wait—and he smiled here and held up his hands—I'm a young guy, I can't wait, I don't have that much control.

He had the sense of things too, he wanted to stave them off or to shift their course, to strike a lighter pitch, but it was a pitch that I couldn't meet anymore, sounding instead a tone more certainly of complaint. I came all the way from Sofia, I said, I've paid for the room, for our meals, for everything, I came to be with you, to have sex with you—and here Mitko broke in, having caught the scent of something he could exploit. Is it just about sex then, he said, you're my friend, using again that word *priyatel* and laying out his own grievances, his own acts of service, having spent so many hours searching through hotels, having reported back to me, having waited in the cold and the rain for me so that now, he said, he felt himself getting sick. He went on for some time, pausing only to drink, as he did often, as though bracing himself for the confrontation he had found he couldn't avoid. But I did all that because we're friends, he said, these are things friends do, it isn't just sex for me. And he paused here more finally, as if he realized he had gone too far, had leaned too hard on the fiction of our relations so that the false surface gave way. But we aren't friends like that, I said, removing the surface altogether as Mitko took another long drink. We get something from it, I said, and the bluntness of the language was now the tool I wanted: I get sex, I said, and you get money. And I felt at once that this was true and at the same time that I had gone too far in my turn, that if Mitko had leaned upon a false surface I was now striking a false depth. And so I softened it, or tried to: I like you, I said, I like being with you, I even said you're dear to me, you're beautiful. But now it was Mitko who insisted on a different tone. His manner had hardened, his manner and his mien, so that the face he wore now was not the face of a few moments before. When have I ever said no to you, he asked, and it was true, though he had delayed and put me off he had never with definiteness refused, he had always when I insisted given in. The trouble with you, he said, darkening further, is that you

"black ice of metaphor" —Merrill

don't know what you want, you say one thing and then another, and he was right, he had caught my own false tones, my search for the appropriate pitch. Nor was it the first time he had caught it, and indeed it was the key of my own peculiar music, this ambivalence that spurs me first to one course of action and then to another, a process of expansion and contraction, so that my entire life, it sometimes seems to me, resembles nothing so much as a kind of grotesquely laboring lung. I offered no resistance to this, I gave even a gesture of acquiescence, at which his manner darkened still further, taking him to a further brink: I'm not like that, he went on, I'm a man of my word, if I say that I'm through with you I'm through, I won't change my mind, and if I see you again, if we pass each other in the street, at NDK, in Plovdiv, in Varna, it doesn't matter where, I'll pretend I don't know you, he said, I won't even say hello. Is that what you want, he said, but not pausing yet for me to respond. Be careful, he said, and there was nothing playful or warm in his aspect now; though he sat naked in front of me he was entirely unavailable. Be sure you tell the truth, be sure you say what you mean. But how could I say what I meant, I thought to myself, when that meaning so entirely escaped me, when I had less a sense of making a choice than of meeting Mitko in his particular music.

I looked at him for a moment, at the length of him folded in the chair; it was a way of delaying an answer but it was also a valedictory look, a drinking in of him with a taste already of remorse. He saw me looking as he poured himself another drink, his third or fourth in a short time, the effects of it were beginning to show, and again I had the thought, but more troubling now, that he was steeling himself for something to come. Well, he said, which is it, and though I hadn't come any closer to a decision or even thought at all in the time he had given me I felt myself pressed to meet his tone, a pressure I was somehow grateful for, a kind of granting of the inevitable. Yes, I said then, yes, I think that's best, but I didn't stop there, I'm sorry, I said, I'm sorry, and then, this is sad for me, *tuzhno mi e*. He looked a moment hard, harder than before, and then he stood up and began pulling on his clothes, moving purposefully but also unsteadily. Think if I were someone else, he said, and there was tension in his voice, he was speaking more quickly and I had to strain to understand him, think if I were a different person, if I were like that guy who stole from you, have you thought about that? Did you think about that when you took me home with you? And there was a new face he bore now, a face I hadn't seen before, a face that became stranger and more unsettling as he continued. I could have been anyone, I could have robbed you, I could have taken your camera and your phone, your computer, I could have hurt you. Did you think of that, he asked again, and he paused, he looked at me so that I could see his new face, which was capable, it seemed to me, of any of those things, and I wondered whether it was a face he had just discovered or perhaps a face he had hidden all along. But we can never know this about such faces, we so seldom look in a way that would let us see them, and even when we do they change so quickly.

I stood up then, feeling the need to assert my own presence, and also to place myself between him and the pile of my belongings I had gathered in one corner; I felt threatened by him, which was what he intended me to feel as he recounted those hypothetical selves. At first it was as though this had its effect, as though he were beating a kind of retreat. But I'm not that sort of person, he said, though this retreat would prove to be simply the first notes of a new theme. If it weren't for me you wouldn't even have them, he went on, stepping up to me where I stood, nobody needed to steal them, you left it all on the bus, and again he gave a little inventory of what I owned, what I had brought with me that might fetch him a few hundred leva in the pawnshops of Varna. Isn't that right, he said, working himself up to the pitch, following his own thread, if it weren't for me you would have lost them anyway, you owe me, and he punctuated this last with a touch, not quite adversarial but aggressive, putting his hand on my shoulder and pressing to see how far I would give way. All the while he held close to my face his new face, a face that frightened me now, not with a debilitating fear but with fear like a light current, a prickling along the nerves. Mitko, I said, softly but I hoped with

confidence, saying his name again as if to call back
the face I knew, Mitko, you should leave now, it's
time for you to leave. He smiled a little at this, he
widened his eyes with amusement and took a half
step away, is it time for me to leave, he said, quoting
my words back to me, is it? And he turned a little
and made a sound, hunh, a sound of puzzlement
and continued amusement, not an angry sound,
and when he turned back his arm swung in a wide
arc and he struck me, with the back of his hand he
struck my face, only once and not terribly hard,
so that when I fell back upon the bed it was as
much from the shock as from the force of it, from
shock and from the passivity that has always been
my instinctive response to violence. We both froze
then, I on the bed and he standing in front of it, as
if both of us were waiting to see what would follow.
Perhaps he felt a kind of passivity too, caught in
something as much as I was caught in fear, real fear
now, physical fear and, strangely enough, already
a kind of narrative fear, as I wondered how badly
I would be bruised and how I would explain it to
my students, fearing the effect of the first light
blow even as I feared the possibility of additional
and heavier ones. I watched Mitko's face, this face
I didn't know and that seemed not to know itself,
that seemed surprised and, I thought, afraid, as if
caught by its own fear, a fear (I imagined) of what it
might do next. It was only an instant that he stood
there, that the coiled tension hung, and then he
moved, he propelled himself forward so that he fell

on top of me, and I must have flinched, I must have shut my eyes though it wasn't his hands I felt then on my face but his mouth, his tongue on the skin of my face as it sought my own mouth, and I opened it without thinking, I let him kiss me though it didn't seem like a kiss, his tongue in my mouth, it was an expression not of tenderness or desire but of violence, as was the weight with which he bore down on me, pinning me to the bed, grinding his chest and then his crotch against mine, then grabbing with one hand my own crotch, gripping it not painfully but commandingly, and I thought whatever happens next I will let it happen. But nothing happened next, he was on me, unbearably present, and then he was gone, he sprang off the bed and left, without taking anything or speaking another word, though of course he could have taken anything at all he wanted.

I lay there for a moment after he left, feeling my fear, which seemed amplified now, so that for a full minute or perhaps for two or three I couldn't force myself to move, even though the door was still open, should anyone from the other rooms have come out they would have seen me there in obvious distress. I lay feeling myself breathe and feeling the pain in my face, not an especially severe pain, perhaps I wouldn't have to invent a story to explain away a bruise, a bruise about which there would certainly be questions, the students would be beside themselves, at least for a moment, the moment before (at the end of the day) I would cease to exist for them. They would already want to know about the trip, about my impressions of the town, of the seashore, as always they would be eager for my opinion of the country; and they knew, too, or hoped they knew, the nature of the friend I was visiting, so that even if they couldn't quite bring themselves to ask they would draw their own conclusions. I got up finally, surprised by how unsteady I felt when so little had happened, when everything was fine, when I was safe now, though as I turned the little latch on the door I realized that in fact I wasn't safe, that the thin tongue of metal between the two wooden wings might easily be forced, it offered really almost no resistance at all. Nor were the windows secure, which also had only single latches where they swung into the room; they were large windows, big enough to pass in or out of, and some of them faced the street, so that one wouldn't even need to enter the courtyard to gain access, by-passing the putative watchman sleeping in his glassed-in porch. I paused then and looked at those windows, realizing that I would be displayed to anyone peering in through the ill-measured drapes, which however I arranged them couldn't be made to cover the entirety of the glass. So the crisis isn't past, I thought to myself, using that word, crisis; I had been right not to feel any relief. I was really frightened then, more frightened than I had been when the threat was more visibly present, when Mitko was in front of me and I knew the worst of it; but then our fantasies are always more vivid than the stuff of life that feeds them, life which always disappoints us until we can embellish it in memory. The crisis wasn't past, and I felt frozen somehow in place, my fear mounting and pinning me where I stood, a feeling I had often had in childhood, when stillness was the only remedy for the terrors I felt at night. It was all I could do to reach out and turn off the lights, listening for any noise outside as I thought again of that face I had seen, that face that was capable of anything and had unaccountably let me off so easy. But perhaps I hadn't been let off so easy, and in light of that face, which seemed to me now of all the faces he had shown Mitko's real face, the others counterfeits and shams, I thought over our other encounters and over, especially, the details of this trip, which he had so carefully arranged. I found myself convinced by improbable thoughts, that Mitko had changed our hotel not because of economy or nearness to the sea, but because of a different sort of convenience altogether, its ease of access and the inadequacy of its locks. I thought of the many friends he had introduced me to, some of whom he had encouraged me to invite into our room, where I would have been, it now occured to me, entirely vulnerable; I thought of the boy he called *brat mi*, who was as steeped in criminality as himself and who would surely be willing to join Mitko in any escapade; I remembered thinking, that first time I saw them together, that he was the passive of the pair, eager to do Mitko whatever service he could.

They were probably together now, I thought to myself, walking the streets as they waited for a later hour. All of Mitko's proposals seemed to me now to have been snares, the invitation to the thermal baths, even to his home among the *blokove*, both of them places where that other face might have had a freer range of action, where Mitko might have become any of the hypothetical selves he had ticked off, might have become all of them at once.

I had convinced myself now, there would be no sleep for me in that room, and so I gathered together my things and went out into the central yard. The attendant, who came out of his little booth to greet me, was the same man who had met us the night before, who had greeted Mitko so warmly and who had surely seen him leave. He was all solicitude when I told him I wanted to change my room, expressing only a slight puzzlement as to why, which I could only explain by saying *ne mi e udobno*, it isn't comfortable for me. He shrugged a little at this and smiled, and then showed me to a much smaller room with a single window looking into the courtyard, looking almost directly at the attendant's porch. He helped me transfer my things, made sure I was satisfied, and then looked at me expectantly, all helpfulness, as if knowing I must have more to say. The man who was with me, I said then, burning with shame to say it, he shouldn't come back here, he isn't welcome, he's not my friend. At this the man's face brightened, not with malice or the scorn I had feared, but with comprehension, simply with knowing now where things stood and also with a sympathy I hadn't expected. I understand completely, he said, don't worry about anything, I'll watch for him and if he shows up here I'll make sure he won't bother you. He paused a moment, he began to leave but then turned back. It's a shame there are such people in the world, he said, you have to be so careful, you pay them, you have your fun, and then they should leave—but sometimes they don't leave, they want more than you agreed. It's a shame, he said again after a pause in which it was clear I had nothing to add, paralyzed in humiliation and wanting only for him to leave. But don't worry, he said again, opening the door, this is a good room—and here he reached over to arrange the curtains so that the glass was entirely covered—you're safe here, don't worry. Then he was gone, finally, and I could lock the door behind him and lie down on the bed, feeling relief now and feeling also despondency and anger, the impotent anger of having been subjected to something, an anger like the dry grinding of gears; perhaps it was an anger that Mitko knew well, that he knew better than I. I felt shame too, a shame I wasn't sure I could account for, a shame I wasn't sure I should accept. And over all of this, over and beneath it at once, I felt an overwhelming fatigue, so that I closed my eyes as I lay there, though it would be a long time before I slept.

I woke early the next morning, despite my desire for sleep, and there was an eerie quality to the light seeping in around the drapes. When I pulled them aside I saw that the air was full of snow, a real shower, though the flakes were fine and nothing as yet was sticking to the ground. In the bathroom I studied my face, tilting it back and forth in the light, and was relieved that the mark it bore was light enough to be mistaken or ignored, so that I didn't need to worry when I stepped out of my room, giving a little wave to the watchman who must have been coming to the end of his shift. Wanting to see the water again, I turned toward the Sea Garden, which wasn't empty despite the hour and the snow; as I walked I passed old couples strolling briskly, men with their dogs, even cyclists, all out for a morning's exercise beside the sea. Just past the entrance on the left there was a huge casino complex, from the depths of which I could hear the driving beat of dance music; there must have been a disco there, where even in the off-season the morning had yet to come. I wanted to see the water, but not just to see it; I wanted if not to touch it to be close to it, to imagine if not to feel the unearthly cold of it. And so I walked more purposefully through the Garden, by-passing, as best I could, its more winding paths, and when I reached again the line of hotels and bars and, beyond them, the road, I didn't retreat from it, I crossed the road and held my face to the wind, though it was biting and filled now with snow, the snow that gave to everything its own peculiar sheen. From the beach there stretched several piers, long walkways extending into the sea, branching at the ends like the arms, it seemed to me, of the flakes of snow sticking to my hair and clothes if not to the ground. I didn't have to walk far to reach one of these walkways, which unlike the park itself was deserted, as the sea was deserted, except for gulls and, far out in the water, two huge tankers that sat unmoving at the horizon. At the start of the pier there was a strange stone sculpture, two stylized figures in robes, who might as easily have been monks as sailors and who seemed to be embracing although they were looking away from each other, each over the other's shoulders, one toward the sea and one toward the shore, an image of irreconcilable desires. The stone was pocked and scarred, already dissolving in the abrasive air, and along its full length the pier, which I walked now, was lined with huge stone objects shaped like jacks from the children's game, a defense against the heavier element of the sea. I walked to the very edge of the pier, to its furthest point, and spent some time looking at these stones and at the interstices between them, where with each wave there surged the white froth of surf. With each contact, I felt the pressure of the water striking the stones and the steadfastness of their resistance, of what seems like their resistance and is simply a slower giving way. The snow was easing now though the wind was still fierce, the air tossed the birds as sharply as the sea. Already I could sense remorse, abstractly and at a certain distance still, but I knew it would be dragged in, that it would turn sharp and terrible, and I accused myself already, thinking bitterly oh, what have I done. Overpoweringly I had the sense, facing that strange element, at once of will-lessness and force, of movement and force against which there could be no lasting defense, what could possibly not crumble before it, so that again it was as if I saw it as it were victorious, the single element unopposed and made one with time, though there would be no meaning to time, when it had washed away before it all intelligence, all witness to its waste triumph. I stood for some time weighing these thoughts, which were dictated more by the measure of the waves than by any active or willed process, until I was chilled beneath my clothes and my face was numb with cold. Then I turned and walked back toward the shore, stamping my feet a little to quicken the sluggish blood.